MW01120977

Discovering Science

SPACE

Rebecca Hunter

RAINTREE
STECK-VAUGHN
PUBLISHERS

A Harcourt Company

Austin   New York
www.steck-vaughn.com

Published by Raintree Steck-Vaughn Publishers, an imprint of Steck-Vaughn Company

Acknowledgments
Project Editors: Rebecca Hunter, Pam Wells
Art Director: Max Brinkmann
Illustrated by Jenny Mumford, Stefan Chabluk, and Keith Williams
Designed by Ian Winton

Planned and produced by Discovery Books

Library of Congress Cataloging-in-Publication Data
Hunter, Rebecca (Rebecca K. de C.)
Space / Rebecca Hunter.
p. cm. -- (Discovering science)
Includes bibliographical references and index.
ISBN 0-7398-3248-4
1. Astronomy--Juvenile literature. [1. Astronomy. 2. Solar system.] I. Title.

QB46 .H86 2001
520--dc21

00-042449

1 2 3 4 5 6 7 8 9 0 BNG 04 03 02 01
Printed and bound in the United States of America.

Note to the reader: You will find difficult words in the glossary on page 30.

CONTENTS

THE NIGHT SKY

Have you ever looked at the sky on a clear night and tried to count the stars? You can probably see hundreds of them, but in fact there are millions. Most stars are so far away that you can't see them at all.

You might think that stars come out only at night. But stars are always there. We cannot see them during the daytime because the sky

is too light. Stars look like tiny specks of light because they are so far away.

It is not just stars that we see in the sky at night. We can often see the Moon, and some of the planets shine brightly enough for us to see them too. If you see something in the night sky that looks like a slow-moving star, it is an artificial satellite.

An astronaut works on the Hubble Space Telescope.

If you were to stay in one place all night and watch the stars, they would seem to move across the sky. It is Earth's rotation that makes the stars appear to move. You can do an experiment to show the pattern of the stars' movement across the sky.

PROJECT

Take a star trail photo

You will need

A camera with time-exposure button

A tripod to hold camera steady

A clear starry night. There must be no Moon and no artificial light.

An adult to help

1. Ask the adult to help you set the camera up on the tripod.

2. Place it in a position outside that has a good, clear view of the sky.

3. Aim the camera at a particularly bright group of stars.

4. Open the shutter on the camera, and leave it for 4 or 5 hours.

5. When you get the film developed, you will be able to see the trails the stars make across the sky. You may need to experiment with the time you leave the camera to see what gives the best results.

STARS

The distances in space are so huge that we measure them in light-years instead of miles. A light-year is the distance a ray of light travels in one year. This is 5.9 trillion miles (9.5 trillion kilometers.) Proxima Centauri, a nearby star, is 4.3 light-years away.

Stars exist in huge groups called galaxies. All the stars we see at night are in a galaxy called the Milky Way. The Milky Way is shaped like a spiral. It measures about 100,000 light-years across.

All the stars we can see are in the Milky Way galaxy.

Do you know what star is nearest to us?
You probably don't think of it as a star at all.
We call it the
Sun. It is still
93 million miles
(150 million
kilometers) away
from us. It
would take you
hundreds of
years to travel
that far in a car!

▶ *The Sun is our nearest star.*

Life on Earth
would not exist
without the Sun.
The light and heat
from the Sun's rays
allow temperatures
on Earth to
support life.

◀ *Living things depend on the Sun.*

THE SUN

Like other stars, the Sun is a huge ball of very hot, glowing gases. It is a million times bigger than Earth. Even so, the Sun isn't particularly big when compared with other stars. Some stars are a million times bigger than the Sun.

The temperature at the surface of the Sun is 10,000°F (5,500°C).

Scientists study the Sun using special telescopes and satellites. This is what the Sun looks like through one of these telescopes.

It has a bright yellow surface with darker patches called sun spots. Sun spots are areas of cooler gas. They look tiny on the Sun's surface, but they are actually many times bigger than Earth.

The huge amount of heat and light that the Sun gives off, travels through space and reaches Earth in about 8 1/3 minutes.

THE SOLAR SYSTEM

The Sun has nine planets that orbit, or move around, it. This is what astronomers call the Solar System. The Solar System also includes the moons that orbit some of the planets and the many asteroids, or pieces of space rock, that form a belt between the planets.

There are two main groups of planets. The inner four, those nearest the Sun, Mercury, Venus, Earth, and Mars are made mostly of rock. The next four, Jupiter, Saturn, Uranus, and Neptune are much larger and are made mostly of gases and liquids. The ninth planet is another small rocky planet called Pluto. It is so far away that we know very little about it.

PROJECT

This model will give you some idea of the relative sizes of the planets in our Solar System.

You will need
Pieces of colored paper
A ruler
A pair of scissors
A set of compasses

1. Using the following scale, cut out circles of paper to represent the nine planets.

	diameter centimeters
Mercury	0.4
Venus	1.0
Earth	1.0
Mars	0.5
Jupiter	11.0
Saturn	9.4
Uranus	4.1
Neptune	3.9
Pluto	0.18

The Sun would be 28 feet in diameter (8.64 meters) using this scale!

2. You can pin your planets on the wall to show their relative sizes.

3. You could make a 3-D model by finding round objects to represent each planet. Earth would be about the size of a marble, and Saturn would be the size of a tennis ball.

ASTEROIDS AND METEORS

Planets and moons are not the only things in the Solar System. There are thousands of pieces of rock called asteroids. Asteroids are rocks that orbit the Sun, just like the other planets. Most of the asteroids are found between Mars and Jupiter. Asteroids range in size from a few feet across to some that are hundreds of miles in diameter.

Every day thousands of pieces of space rock and other matter fall toward Earth. Most of these pieces burn up as they fly through the atmosphere. We call these streaks of light meteors, or "shooting stars."

Sometimes a large rock survives passing through the atmosphere and falls to the ground as a meteorite. Most meteorites are quite small, but Earth shows it was hit by some very large meteorites.

Meteor Crater in Arizona, measures 0.8 miles (1.3 kilometers) across. It was formed about 25,000 years ago when a meteorite about 150 feet (45 m) across hit Earth.

COMETS

A comet is a mountain-sized lump of snow, ice, and gas. There are millions of comets orbiting the Sun. Usually they are too far away for us to see them. When a comet comes close to the Sun, some of its snow and ice turns into gas. This gas streams out behind the comet and is called its "tail." A comet looks like a star with a tail. It appears in the sky for a few weeks.

Most comets are seen only once, but some return on a regular schedule. Halley's Comet returns every 76 years.

This is the comet Hale Bopp which passed by Earth in 1997.

THE PLANETS

THE INNER PLANETS

Mercury is a small rocky planet. At 36 million miles (58 million kilometers) it is the closest planet to the Sun. Mercury takes 88 days to go once around the Sun. This is a "year" on Mercury.

HAPPY BIRTHDAY!
Just imagine! If you lived on Mercury, you would have a birthday every 3 months!

However, nobody could live on Mercury. Because it is so close to the Sun, it gets very hot. Its daytime temperature is about 806°F (430°C). At night it gets very cold with temperatures much lower than anything we experience on Earth.

The surface of Mercury shows many craters from meteorites that have hit it.

VENUS

Venus is a rocky planet that is about the same size as Earth. However, conditions on Venus are very different from those on Earth. Venus is very hot and its atmosphere is poisonous. The surface of Venus is hidden by swirling clouds of sulfuric acid droplets. Under the clouds, the atmosphere is composed almost completely of carbon dioxide. There is no oxygen.

Venus looks like a bright star in the sky. It is known as the "evening star," because it can often be seen from Earth in the early evening before it gets dark. It is also called the "morning star," because it can sometimes be seen in the early morning before it gets light.

This picture of Venus was obtained from the Magellan mission in 1989.

EARTH

Earth is the third planet from the Sun and is very unlike all the others in the Solar System. Earth is the only planet known to support life. There are three important factors that allow this. The temperature is just right, liquid water is available, and the atmosphere contains oxygen.

Seen from space, Earth is a mass of blue, green, and white.

Three-fourths of Earth is covered with water. The land appears green and the atmosphere can be seen as swirls of white clouds. Earth has a single satellite, the Moon, which is about one-fourth the size of the planet.

MARS

Mars is sometimes known as the "red planet" because it is a reddish-brown color. Mars has two tiny moons, Phobos and Deimos. These were probably asteroids that were captured by Mars' gravity. For a while people thought there might be life on Mars. But Mars is a cold, hostile planet.

We cannot breathe in Mars' atmosphere. Huge dust storms rage on the surface. Mars has been visited by several space probes that have taken pictures of the planet. They show that much of the surface is a stony desert.

Photographs from Mars show a red and rocky surface.

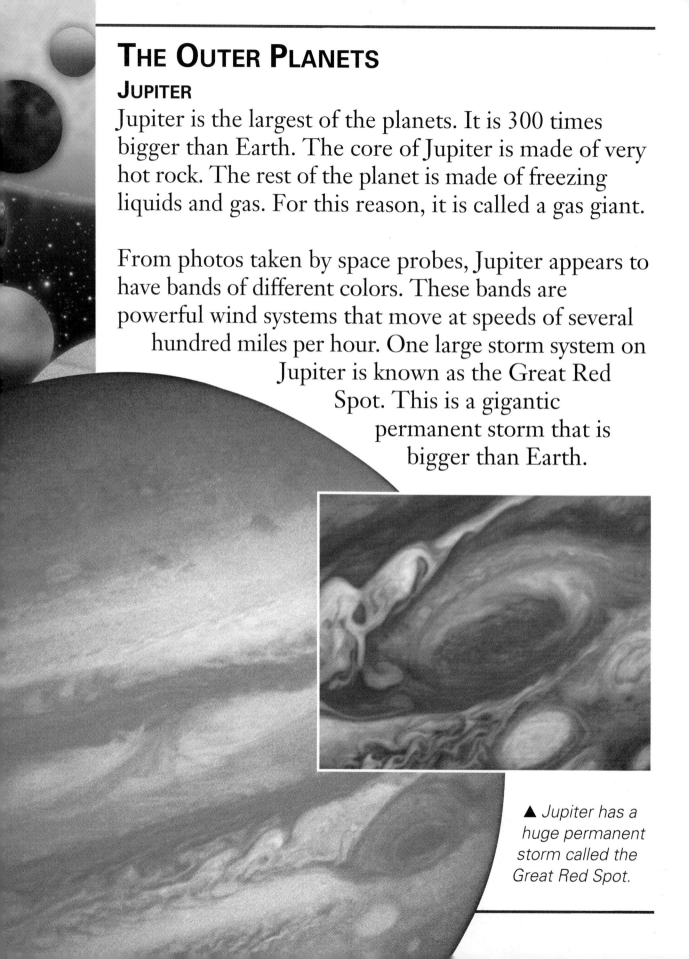

THE OUTER PLANETS

JUPITER

Jupiter is the largest of the planets. It is 300 times bigger than Earth. The core of Jupiter is made of very hot rock. The rest of the planet is made of freezing liquids and gas. For this reason, it is called a gas giant.

From photos taken by space probes, Jupiter appears to have bands of different colors. These bands are powerful wind systems that move at speeds of several hundred miles per hour. One large storm system on Jupiter is known as the Great Red Spot. This is a gigantic permanent storm that is bigger than Earth.

▲ *Jupiter has a huge permanent storm called the Great Red Spot.*

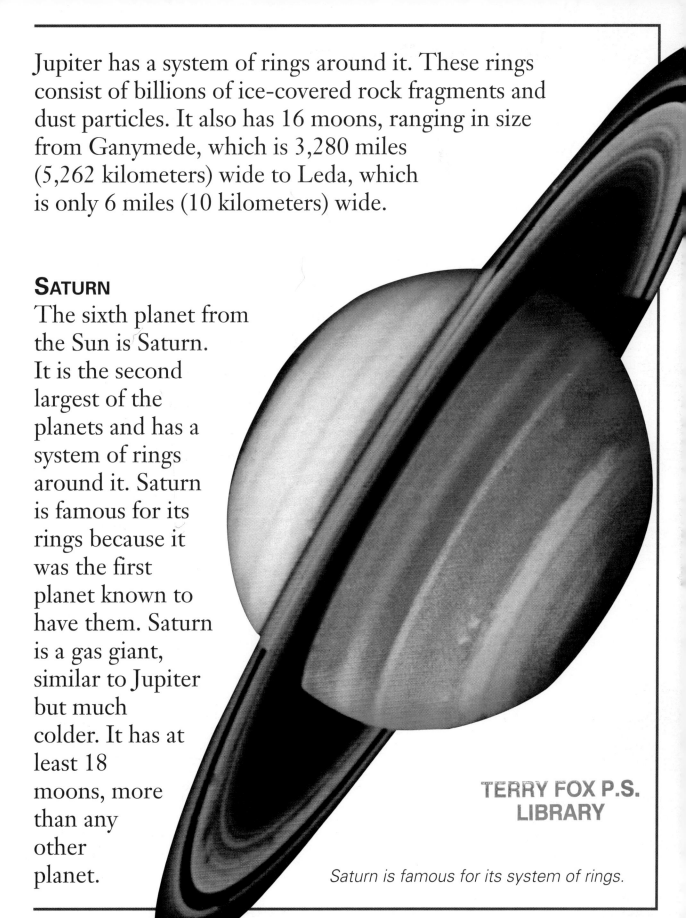

Jupiter has a system of rings around it. These rings consist of billions of ice-covered rock fragments and dust particles. It also has 16 moons, ranging in size from Ganymede, which is 3,280 miles (5,262 kilometers) wide to Leda, which is only 6 miles (10 kilometers) wide.

SATURN

The sixth planet from the Sun is Saturn. It is the second largest of the planets and has a system of rings around it. Saturn is famous for its rings because it was the first planet known to have them. Saturn is a gas giant, similar to Jupiter but much colder. It has at least 18 moons, more than any other planet.

Saturn is famous for its system of rings.

URANUS

Uranus is 1,722 million miles (2,870 million km) from the Sun. Light from the Sun takes two and one-half hours to reach it. It takes 84 of our years for Uranus to orbit the Sun. If you lived there, you might never have your first birthday!

Uranus is another cold, gas giant. Photographs of the planet show clouds of frozen methane gas that make the planet look blue. Uranus also has rings. You can see 11 rings in photos. They are made of rocks about 40 inches (1 meter) across.

DID YOU KNOW?
Uranus has at least 15 moons that are all (except one) named after characters in William Shakespeare's plays!

Neptune

Neptune is the farthest away of the gas planets and is similar to Uranus. It also looks blue in color and has a ring system and eight moons. One of Neptune's moons, Triton, is the coldest place in the Solar System. Neptune also has the fastest winds in the Solar System, and many violent storms rage on its surface. Only one space probe has visited Uranus and Neptune. This was *Voyager 2*, and the journey took 12 years to complete.

Neptune has a ring system and eight moons.

Pluto

Because it is so far away, not much is known about Pluto. It has one large moon called Charon. Scientists believe that both Pluto and Charon consist of rocky cores with an icy covering of water and methane. A year on Pluto lasts 248 Earth years.

THE MOON

The Moon is a natural satellite of Earth. Nobody is quite sure where the Moon came from. It may be a piece of Earth that broke away millions of years ago. It is more likely that it was formed at the same time as Earth, about 4.5 billion years ago.

The Moon is made of rock. Because of the way it rotates, the same side of the Moon always faces the Earth. The other side that we don't see is known as "the dark side of the Moon." The Moon surface is covered with large mountains and flat areas called maria. Years ago people thought these areas might be seas.

There are also many craters that were formed by large rocks or asteroids crashing into the Moon millions of years ago. Nothing lives on the Moon. There is no water here and no atmosphere. Temperatures range from very hot during the day, 260°F (126°C), to freezing cold at night, -280°F (-173°C).

The Moon is always there in the sky, but it is much easier to see it at night. It does not produce its own light, but reflects the Sun's light, like a mirror.

The Moon takes just over 29 days to orbit Earth. As it does this we see different shapes according to the amount of the sunlit side that is visible.

PROJECT

Record the phases of the Moon.

Remember that sometimes you can see the Moon during the day rather than at night. Sometimes it will be too cloudy to see the Moon at all.

You will need
A large piece of paper
A pencil

1. Draw 8 circles on the paper.

2. Look at the Moon one evening and draw the shape you see in the first of the circles.

3. Three days later, look at the Moon again and draw the shape in the next circle.

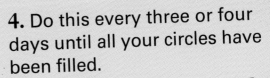

4. Do this every three or four days until all your circles have been filled.

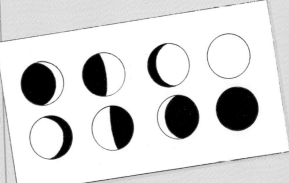

Look at the Moon on the 29th day. What shape is it now?

LUNAR LANDINGS

The Moon is our closest neighbor in space. It is about 238,000 miles (380,000 km) away and people have been studying it for thousands of years. Early people dreamed of reaching the Moon using birds or balloons. However it was not until 1959 that the first spacecraft crash-landed on the Moon. The first controlled landing was the Soviet *Luna 9*, in 1966, which sent back the first pictures of the surface.

In 1969 the United States sent a spacecraft named *Apollo 11* to the Moon. Three astronauts were on board, Neil Armstrong, Edwin, "Buzz," Aldrin, and Michael Collins. They had all spent months training for the journey, which was the first to put a person on the Moon.

Neil Armstrong, the first person on the Moon. Over 600 million people, a fifth of the world's population, watched this event on television.

When Neil Armstrong stepped out of Apollo onto the Moon's surface on July 20, he said a sentence that has become famous: "That's one small step for a man, one giant leap for mankind."

The astronauts had to wear specially designed spacesuits to provide them with air and keep them warm. There is much less gravity on the Moon than on Earth, so everything feels lighter and astronauts can move around in great leaps.

Because there is no atmosphere and no weather on the Moon, the footprints they left will remain forever.

After 1969, five other Apollo missions landed people on the Moon. Scientists are now discussing building a permanent space center on the Moon, where they can live and work for several months at a time. They may even build a hotel on the Moon so that people can take vacations there!

LOOKING AT SPACE

CONSTELLATIONS

Throughout history, people all over the world have looked out to space and made up stories to explain where the stars came from. They gave names to groups, or constellations, of stars that we still use today. Astronomers have identified 88 constellations. The stars in these groups are not actually related in any way and may be huge distances apart.

The Big Dipper is a group of stars that is easy to see. It is part of the constellation known as the Great Bear (Ursa Major). Some people think it looks like a large saucepan! The two stars forming the side of the pan in the Big Dipper point to a star called the North Star. That star always points to the North Pole. The North Star is very useful to sailors navigating at sea.

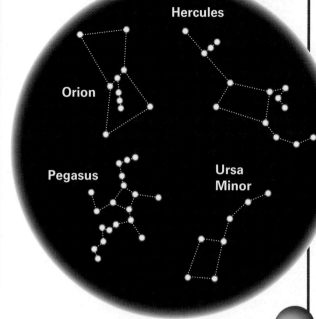

Hercules

Orion

Pegasus

Ursa Minor

▲ *This group of stars is called Orion.*

PROJECT

Make your own constellations

You will need
A cardboard tube
Some black paper
A pin
A pair of scissors
A rubber band
A set of compasses

1. Cut out some circles of paper, slightly larger than the end of the tube.

2. With a pin, make small holes in the circles to form patterns of stars.

Copy the constellations shown above.

3. Fix the paper circle over the end of the tube with the rubber band.

4. Hold the tube up to the light and look through it to see the star constellation.

When you are familiar with the star constellations, why not try and find them in the sky?

SATELLITES AND TELESCOPES

Scientists get information about Earth, the Sun, and the rest of the Universe by using telescopes, satellites, and space probes.

There are thousands of artificial satellites in orbit around Earth. They send back pictures that can help predict our weather, and they look out for signs of pollution on Earth.

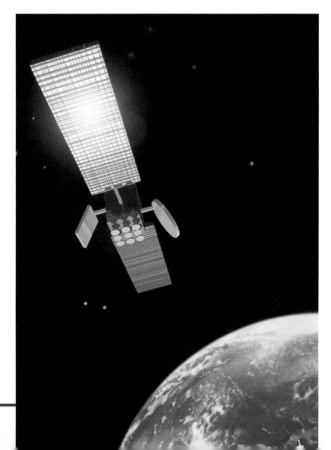

This is a satellite. It is in orbit around Earth.

SPACECRAFT

The Space Shuttle was the first spacecraft that could be used more than once. It is launched into space with two booster rockets. These are released after takeoff and recovered. The shuttle can carry eight people and equipment into space. When it returns, it lands like an aircraft.

The exploration of outer space goes on. Unmanned craft have already been to Mars, Saturn, and Jupiter. Some have even sent back pictures of distant planets such as Uranus and Neptune. Some astronomers think there may still be an undiscovered planet in our Solar System. They call this planet, Planet X.

The Universe is so vast, and the distances between planets, stars and galaxies is so great, that it will probably be some time before astronauts ever set foot on other planets. Exploration beyond our Solar System is even less likely to happen. It would take our fastest spaceship 80,000 years to reach the nearest star!

GLOSSARY

astronaut A crew member of a spacecraft.

astronomer A person who studies space.

atmosphere A blanket of gases around a planet.

constellation A group of stars that are named after the pattern they make when seen from Earth. Some are named after animals.

galaxy A huge group of stars. The Milky Way is our galaxy. The Sun and our solar system are in the Milky Way.

gravity A force that pulls objects toward each other.

light-year The distance light travels in one year.

moon A small body that orbits a planet.

orbit The path of one object around another.

planet A large, ball-shaped object that orbits a star.

satellite An object that orbits a planet or moon.

space probe A robot spacecraft sent out to explore space.

star A huge, glowing ball of gas in space.

universe All the stars, planets, moons, and galaxies in space, and the space between them.

FURTHER READING

Branley, Franklyn. *Planets in Our Solar System*. (Let's-Read-and-Find-Out Science Book). HarperCollins, 1981.

Silver, Donald M. *Night Sky*. (One Small Square series). McGraw, 1998.

Sims, Lesley. *Moon*. (What About...? series). Raintree Steck-Vaughn Co., 1994.

Sims, Lesley. *Sun and Stars*. (What About...? series). Raintree Steck-Vaughn Co., 1994.

Tompkins, Pat. *Stars*. Monday Morning Books, 1999

Walker, Jane. *Solar System*. (Fascinating Facts series). Millbrook Press, 1995.

The publishers would like to thank the following for permission to reproduce their pictures:

Bruce Coleman: page 5, 7 bottom, 10, 13, 19 (Francico Futil), 20, 21, 27, 28 top, Cover; **gettyone Stone**: page 7 top (Eastcott), 17 top, 22 bottom, 26, 28 bottom; **NASA**: page 4 bottom, 15, 16, 18 inset, 22, top, 24 top, 25, 29; **Science Photo Library**: page 4 top (Frank Zullo), 6 (Allan Morton), 9, 12 (David Parker), 14 (US Geo Survey), 17 bottom (NASA), 18 (NASA), 24 inset (NASA).

INDEX